CLASSIC RIDES

CLASSIC Porsches

BY CLAIRE ROMAINE

INVESTIGATE!

Enslow PUBLISHING

Please visit our website, www.enslow.com. For a free color catalog of all our high-quality books, call toll free 1-800-398-2504 or fax 1-877-980-4454.

Library of Congress Cataloging-in-Publication Data

Names: Romaine, Claire, author.
Title: Classic Porsches / Claire Romaine.
Description: New York : Enslow Publishing, [2021] | Series: Classic rides | Includes index.
Identifiers: LCCN 2019054696 | ISBN 9781978518094 (library binding) | ISBN 9781978518070 (paperback) | ISBN 9781978518087 (6 Pack) | ISBN 9781978518100 (ebook)
Subjects: LCSH: Porsche automobiles–Juvenile literature.
Classification: LCC TL215.P75 R66 2021 | DDC 629.222–dc23
LC record available at https://lccn.loc.gov/2019054696

Published in 2021 by
Enslow Publishing
101 West 23rd Street, Suite #240
New York, NY 10011

Designer: Katelyn E. Reynolds
Editor: Therese Shea

Photo credits: Cover, p. 1 (left Porsche) Everyonephoto Studio/Shutterstock.com; cover, p. 1 (middle Porsche) Radoslaw Lecyk/Shutterstock.com; cover, p. 1 (right Porsche) Dariusz Majgier/Shutterstock.com; cover, pp. 1–32 (series chrome font) Mott Jordan/Shutterstock.com; cover, pp. 1–32 (series background) Sylvie Bouchard/Shutterstock.com; p. 5 (inset) r.classen/Shutterstock; p. 5 (main) Alexander Kirch/Shutterstock; p. 7 Ptyx/Wikipedia.org; pp. 8, 9, 10, 17 (main), 18 Car Culture, Inc./Car Culture ® Collection/Getty Images Plus; p. 11 Matti Blume/Wikipedia.org; p. 12 Heritage Images/Hulton Archive/Getty Images; p. 13 Jean-Claude Deutsch/Paris Match via Getty Images; p. 14 National Motor Museum/Heritage Images via Getty Images; p. 15 Andrei Bortnikau/Shutterstock; p. 17 (inset) contrastaddict/iStock Unreleased/Getty Images; p. 19 (both) RikoBest/Shutterstock; p. 21 Ker Robertson/Getty Images; p. 23 Gerlach Delissen/Corbis via Getty Images; p. 24 Daria Trefilova/Shutterstock; p. 25 Andrew Burton/Getty Images; p. 26 Axel Koester/Corbis via Getty Images; p. 27 Roman Belogorodov/Shutterstock; p. 29 Atilgan Ozdil/Anadolu Agency/Getty Images.

Portions of this work were originally authored by Heather Moore Niver and published as *Porsches*. All new material in this edition authored by Claire Romaine.

Printed in the United States of America

Some of the images in this book illustrate individuals who are models. The depictions do not imply actual situations or events.

CPSIA compliance information: Batch #BS20ENS: For further information contact Enslow Publishing, New York, New York, at 1-800-398-2504.

Contents

WORDS IN THE GLOSSARY APPEAR IN **BOLD** TYPE THE FIRST TIME THEY ARE USED IN THE TEXT.

A CAR TO Admire

Just the name "Porsche" has commanded the respect and admiration of car fans for decades. Porsche **engineers** have the highest standards for the vehicles that bear the Porsche emblem, or symbol. These cars have a sleek style that many sports cars try to copy. They also perform like they were made for the racetrack—and some were!

GET THE FACTS!

The Porsche emblem shows a horse as the symbol of Stuttgart, Germany, where Porsche manufactures its cars. (Stuttgart was built on a horse farm.) Antlers and red and black stripes stand for the old Kingdom of Württemberg, Germany.

Porsches are perfect examples of classic cars. They're of the highest quality, and many become more valuable as they age. Every model has fans who are eager to add it to their collection.

ARE YOU SAYING "PORSCHE" CORRECTLY? MANY PEOPLE DON'T! IT'S PRONOUNCED "POR-SHUH."

PORSCHE 911

Beginnings

The name "Porsche" comes from Ferdinand Porsche, an early car **designer** from the area in Europe now called the Czech Republic. He worked for the Jacob Lohner carriage company in the late 1800s. Carriages are carts with wheels in which people ride. Porsche built an electric carriage for the World's Fair in Paris, France, in 1900. It was called the System Lohner-Porsche.

GET THE FACTS!

In 1934, the Porsche company designed tractors. Porsche tractors used the same kind of engine for every model until the last one in 1963. During World War II, Ferdinand and his son Ferry worked on tank designs for Germany too.

THE SYSTEM LOHNER-PORSCHE IS CONSIDERED THE FIRST HYBRID BECAUSE ITS ENGINE RAN ON BOTH GAS AND ELECTRICITY.

Ferdinand Porsche designed for the Volkswagen car company in the 1930s and began his own business in 1931. When the first Porsche model was produced, it was based heavily on the Volkswagen.

THE FIRST Porsches

The Porsche company focused on race cars and sports cars. On June 8, 1948, the first true Porsche car, the 356, was approved for roads. It's sometimes called the cousin of the Volkswagen Beetle because they looked so similar. They both had engines cooled by air located in the rear of the car too.

BY THE END OF 1955, PORSCHE HAD PRODUCED MORE THAN 7,600 OF THE PORSCHE 356.

1957 PORSCHE 356 SPEEDSTER CONVERTIBLE

In the early 1950s, Porsche introduced a 356 model called the Speedster. Drivers could choose a **coupe** or a **convertible**. The coupes had hard tops, and the convertibles, which they called cabriolets, had soft tops.

GET THE FACTS!

To celebrate its 60th anniversary, Porsche searched for the oldest Porsches sold in America. The winner was a 1952 Porsche 356 Cabriolet owned by a man in Oklahoma. A 1950 356 Cabriolet was found in Maryland, but it had been brought to the United States from Germany.

911s

1970 PORSCHE 911 TARGA

In 1963, Porsche introduced the 911. It has been making this model ever since! The body style has changed through the years, but the engine has remained in the rear. The 1967 911 Targa featured a **roll bar** beneath a steel cover. The top between the roll bar and the windshield could be removed.

GET THE FACTS!

In 1975, Porsche added another edition of the 911—the Turbo Carrera. Porsche added a turbocharger, a device to increase engine power. It worked! The car was so different from the 911 that it was given its own number: 930.

The 2020 model of the Porsche 911 Carrera can go from 0 to 60 miles (97 km) per hour in 4 seconds. It also boasts 379 **horsepower** and a top speed of 182 miles (293 km) per hour!

IN 2017, THE ONE-MILLIONTH PORSCHE 911 WAS PRODUCED!

914s

In 1969, Porsche worked with Volkswagen to roll out a car that more people could afford. Starting at around $3,500, this vehicle, the 914, offered a Volkswagen engine with just 80 horsepower. It had a mid-engine design, which meant the engine was right behind the driver and passenger. This model wasn't received well. Some didn't even consider it a "real" Porsche.

The model called the 914/6 included a Porsche engine. However, it didn't sell well either because it was too expensive. The last 914s were made in 1976.

GET THE FACTS!

Mid-engine cars were popular on the racetrack when the 914 was introduced. However, an engine produces a lot of heat, noise, and movement, and there wasn't much padding between the engine and the passengers. That was one reason it wasn't successful.

928s and 944s

In 1978, Porsche offered a model called the 928. The company believed it might replace the 911. This lightweight Porsche was the first model designed with the engine in the front of the car. It also had an eight-**cylinder**, or V-8, engine. However, the 928s never became as popular as the 911s. Production halted in 1995.

1980 PORSCHE 928

GET THE FACTS!

Many car companies are owned by a larger company. For example, Chevrolet, or Chevy, is owned by General Motors (GM). Porsche has always been proud to be an independent car company. That means it has total control over its designs and production.

In 1982, the first 944s hit the highways. A Porsche-built four-cylinder engine moved it from 0 to 60 miles (97 km) per hour in less than 6 seconds. It reached a top speed of 155 miles (249 km) per hour.

SOME PEOPLE DIDN'T THINK THE PORSCHE 928 WAS A "TRUE" PORSCHE BECAUSE OF THE EIGHT-CYLINDER ENGINE. THE 944, WHICH HAD A FOUR-CYLINDER ENGINE, WAS ONLY PRODUCED UNTIL 1991.

PORSCHE 944

Boxsters

In the 1990s, the Porsche company wasn't doing well. Its cars weren't selling—until the Boxster was introduced in 1996. This two-seater had a six-cylinder engine cooled with water, which was known as a "boxer." A roadster is a two-door open car. Porsche combined "boxer" and "roadster" to come up with the name. The Boxster reminded car lovers of the classic Porsches from the 1950s.

GET THE FACTS!

The Porsche Cayman is a coupe modeled after the Boxster. The name "Cayman" refers to an alligator-like reptile from Central and South America. Like the Boxster, the Cayman is a mid-engine car designed to be more affordable.

Encouraged by the Boxster's success, Porsche produced more powerful models. The 2020 718 Boxster speeds from 0 to 60 miles (97 km) per hour in 4.9 seconds!

THE BOXSTER WAS THE AFFORDABLE PORSCHE THAT PEOPLE HAD BEEN WAITING FOR. IT'S STILL IN PRODUCTION. TODAY'S BOXSTERS COME WITH A 300-HORSEPOWER ENGINE.

1997 PORSCHE BOXSTER

ENTER THE SUV

In 2001, Porsche introduced its Cayenne, a **sport utility vehicle** (SUV). Many Porsche sports car fans were unhappy that the model—named after a hot pepper—was even offered. However, the company wanted to expand its offerings to customers who needed something other than a two-door sports car.

GET THE FACTS!

In 2011, Porsche introduced a hybrid Cayenne model. The hybrid engine didn't affect its high performance. Recent Cayenne Turbo S E-Hybrids offer as much as 670 horsepower and a top track speed of 183 miles (295 km) per hour!

Although it was less sleek than a sports car, the Cayenne was sturdy. It had more space than other Porsches but was smaller than other mid-size SUVs. Its excellent steering and **all-wheel drive** appealed to sports-car fans. The Cayenne offered several different engines for a range of power.

PORSCHE CAYENNE TURBO S E-HYBRID COUPE

THE CAYENNE WAS FIRST OFFERED IN EUROPE IN 2001 AND THEN IN NORTH AMERICA IN 2003.

SPEED AND Endurance

Company founder Ferdinand Porsche had a love for race cars. Almost every series model has started out as a race car, so unsurprisingly, Porsches have always been on the race track. They have had success especially in long-distance races, such as the 24 Hours of Le Mans. Porsche has had 19 victories in this 24-hour competition as of 2019.

GET THE FACTS!

In 2018, FIA accepted Porsche's application to manufacture electric race cars for the Formula E race series. Formula E was created to show that races could be just as exciting with all-electric race cars, which, unlike gas-powered race cars, produce no air pollution.

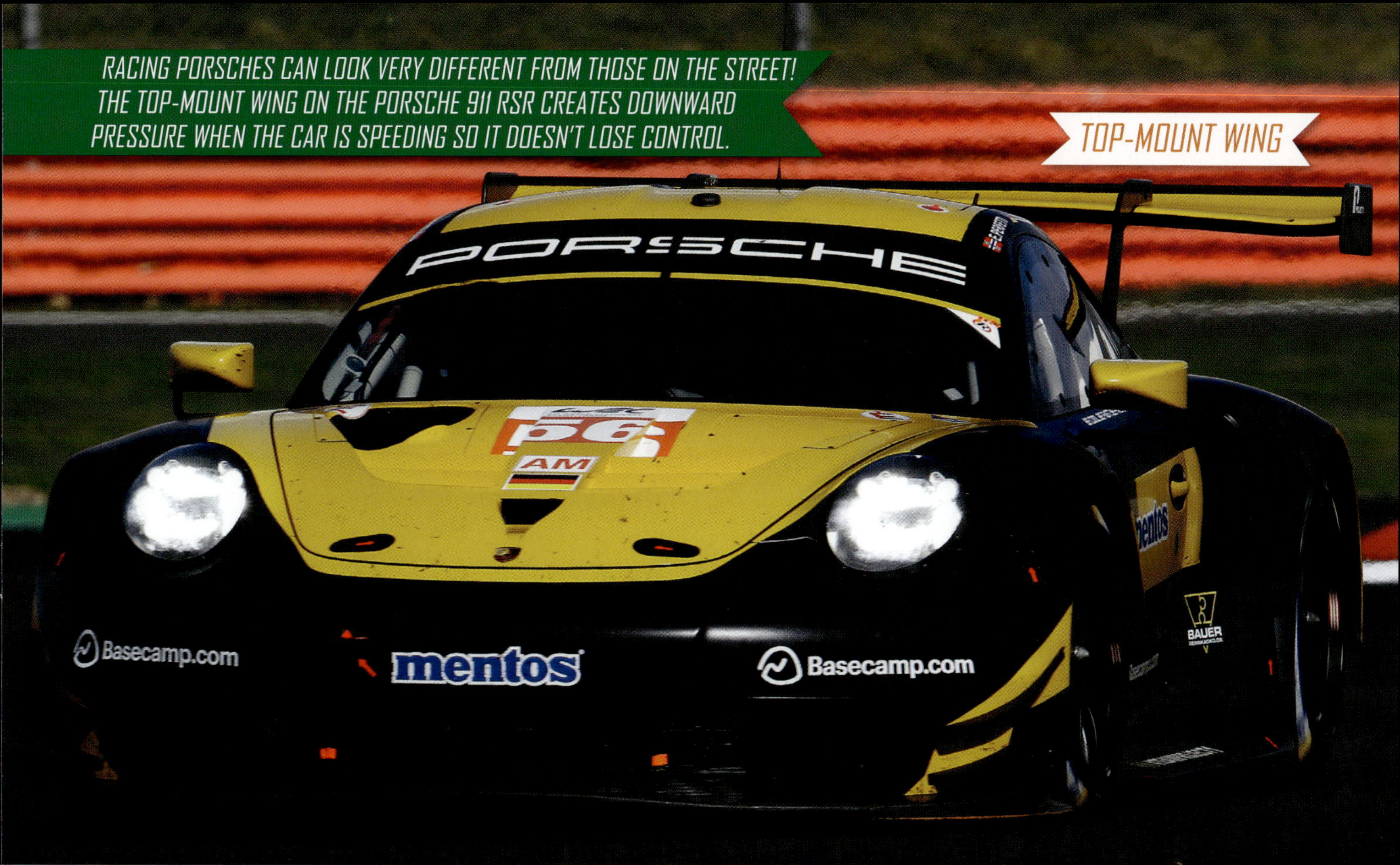

RACING PORSCHES CAN LOOK VERY DIFFERENT FROM THOSE ON THE STREET! THE TOP-MOUNT WING ON THE PORSCHE 911 RSR CREATES DOWNWARD PRESSURE WHEN THE CAR IS SPEEDING SO IT DOESN'T LOSE CONTROL.

Porsche teams also won three victories in a row in the FIA (Fédération Internationale de l'Automobile) World Endurance Championship, from 2015 to 2017. These races are at least six hours long.

AN Anniversary

In 2019, Porsche announced it would be honoring the 50th anniversary of Porsche's first win at the 24 Hours of Le Mans in 1970. It created an exhibit at the Porsche Museum in Stuttgart, Germany.

Porsche designers also created a special model called the 917 Living Legend to honor the car that won the 24 Hours of Le Mans. Like the 1970 917K, it has a wedge-like nose, low hood, and large front **fenders**. It's also like the 918 Spyder, with its rectangular headlights and front air intakes.

GET THE FACTS!

People who want the 917's speed off the track might choose the 918 Spyder, a hybrid with over 800 horsepower. With a special **options package**, this "supercar" can go from 0 to 60 miles (97 km) in 2.5 seconds!

DO YOU LIKE THE LOOK OF THE 918 SPYDER? PRICES START AT OVER $800,000!

FASTEST PORSCHES OFF THE TRACK

MODEL	TIME IT TAKES TO REACH 60 MILES (97 KM) PER HOUR	TOP SPEED (MILES PER HOUR)
911 TURBO S	2.8 SECONDS	205
CARRERA GT	3.5 SECONDS	207
959 S	3.7 SECONDS	211
911 GT2 RS	2.6 SECONDS	211
918 SPYDER	2.5 SECONDS	214

PORSCHES IN Music

Classic cars—including Porsches—have been the subject of many songs. Famous soul and blues singer Janis Joplin sang, "My friends all drive Porsches." Joplin had one too. She painted her 1964 356 C Cabriolet in the colors popular in the 1960s.

1952 PORSCHE 356 1500 SUPER

GET THE FACTS!

Soon after the first Porsche arrived in the United States, its design caught the eye of the art world. In 1953, the Museum of Modern Art in New York City included a 1952 Porsche 1500 Super in one of its exhibits.

JANIS JOPLIN'S FAMOUS CAR HAS BEEN ON DISPLAY AT DIFFERENT ART AND AUTO MUSEUMS ALL OVER THE UNITED STATES.

In the song "Parents Just Don't Understand," Will Smith and DJ Jazzy Jeff rapped about sneaking out late one night in Smith's parents' Porsche. Lil Wayne, Nelly, Jay-Z, and Kendrick Lamar all have songs with lyrics about Porsches as well. Porsches show up in rock, country, and R & B songs too!

PORSCHES IN Movies

Porsches have both looks and speed. They're featured in movies for just these reasons. In the 1971 movie *Le Mans*, actor and race-car enthusiast Steve McQueen drives a Porsche 917K. He races against another driver in a Ferrari 512 LM.

GET THE FACTS!

Comedian Jerry Seinfeld owns more Porsches than anyone else. At one time he may have had as many as 47, though he has sold some at **auctions**. Among his models, he has one of only 200 Porsche 959s made.

In the *Cars* film series, the character Sally Carrera is a light blue 2002 Porsche 911. According to Pixar, Sally has a six-cylinder rear engine and can reach speeds up to 177 miles (285 km) per hour! That's almost as fast as her friend Lightning McQueen, a Corvette-like car.

THIS ACTUAL 2002 PORSCHE 911 HAS BEEN MADE TO LOOK LIKE PIXAR'S SALLY CARRERA. IT CAN BE VIEWED AT THE PORSCHE MUSEUM IN GERMANY.

CLASSICS to Come

The Porsche car company is poised to remain among the leading makers of sports cars into the future. It hasn't been afraid to change over the years, offering more affordable cars and larger vehicles, to reflect the needs of car buyers.

The classic Porsche 911 is a lasting reminder of the brand's past as well as its continuing success into the future. Newer versions of the model are still in demand today. Drivers looking for a high-performance vehicle will find just what they want in the seat of a Porsche!

GET THE FACTS!

Recent cars added to the Porsche family include the all-electric Taycan, the full-sized Panamera ***sedan****, and the small SUV called the Macan. Each is offered as several different models so customers can find the right driving experience for them.*

PORSCHE DRIVERS CAN JOIN SPECIAL CLUBS TO GET IN TOUCH WITH OTHER PORSCHE OWNERS. THEY HAVE CAR SHOWS AND EVEN RACES!

MOST EXPENSIVE PORSCHES SOLD AT AUCTION

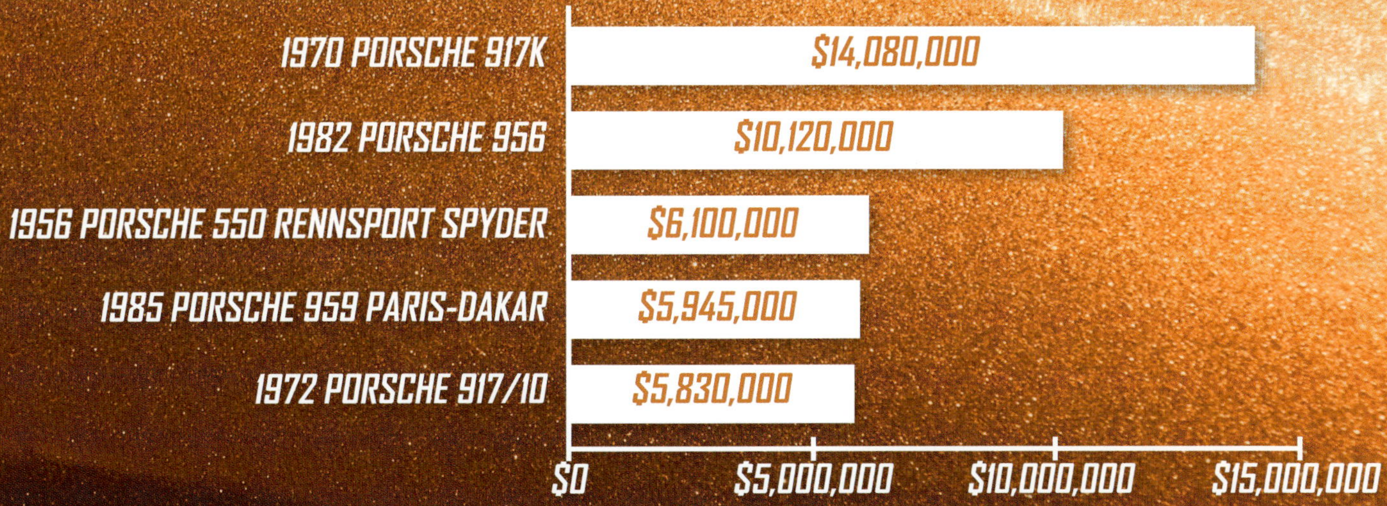

Glossary

all-wheel drive A system of moving a car that powers all four wheels instead of just the front or back wheels.

auction A sale of goods or property at which buyers bid against one another for items.

convertible A car with a roof that can be lowered or removed.

coupe A two-door car with one section for the seats and another for storage space.

cylinder A tube-shaped space in an engine in which a piston is pushed by the pressure or force of a fluid.

designer Someone who creates the plan or form of something. A design is the plan or form itself.

engineer Someone who plans and builds machines.

fender Any of the corner parts of the body of a car, especially those that surround the wheels.

horsepower A unit used to measure the power of an engine.

import A product brought into a country to be sold there.

options package A group of choices for a car bundled together and offered at a single price.

roll bar An overhead metal bar on an automobile that helps protect the driver in case of a rollover.

sedan A car with front and back seats, two or four doors, an enclosed body, and a permanent top.

sport utility vehicle A car similar to a station wagon but built on a light-truck frame.

FOR MORE INFORMATION

BOOKS

Cruz, Calvin. *Porsche 918 Spyder*. Minneapolis, MN: Bellwether Media, 2016.

Kingston, Seth. *The History of Porsches*. New York, NY: PowerKids Press, 2019.

Piddock, Charles. *Porsche 911*. North Mankato, MN: Rourke Educational Media, 2017.

WEBSITES

Porsche
www.porsche.com/usa/
Read about the newest Porsche models.

Porsche Milestones
www.porsche.com/museum/en/milestones/
Check out this timeline of the company's history.

Publisher's note to educators and parents: Our editors have carefully reviewed these websites to ensure that they are suitable for students. Many websites change frequently, however, and we cannot guarantee that a site's future contents will continue to meet our high standards of quality and educational value. Be advised that students should be closely supervised whenever they access the internet.

Index